INSIDE-OUT GRANDMA

INSIDE-OUT GRANDMA

Joan Rothenberg

Hyperion Books for Children
New York

Text and illustrations © 1995 by Joan Rothenberg.
All rights reserved.
Printed in Hong Kong by South China Printing Co. (1988) Ltd.
For information address Hyperion Books for Children,
114 Fifth Avenue, New York, New York 10011.

3 5 7 9 10 8 6 4

Library of Congress Cataloging-in-Publication Data
Rothenberg, Joan
Inside-out grandma / Joan Rothenberg—1st ed.
p.   cm.
Summary: Rosie's grandmother wears her clothes inside out to
remind herself to buy oil for making latkes at Hanukkah.
Includes a recipe for potato latkes.
ISBN 0-7868-0107-7 (trade)—ISBN 0-7868-2092-6 (lib. bdg.)
[1. Grandmothers—Fiction.   2. Hanukkah—Fiction.   3. Judaism—
Customs and practices—Fiction.   4. Jews—United States—Fiction.]
I. Title.
PZ7.R7425In   1995   [E]—dc20   94-23677
The artwork for each picture is prepared using gouache and pencil.
This book is set in 16-point Esprit Book.

For my mom and dad,
who taught me
that there's no such
thing as a
Hanukkah bush!

I love you
xxxxxxxx

G randma," said Rosie, "do you know that you have your clothes on inside out?"

"I certainly do," answered Grandma.

"You look so silly!" giggled Rosie.

"I may look silly to you, my little Rosie Posie, but I have an excellent reason. Hanukkah is coming soon and I have to remind myself to buy enough oil to fry the potato latkes."

"How does wearing inside-out clothes remind you to buy enough oil to fry the potato latkes?" asked Rosie.

"When I wear my clothes inside out, it reminds me of your daddy. That boy was always in such a hurry. Half the time he had his clothes on inside out and sometimes even backwards!"

"But how do my daddy and wearing inside-out clothes help you to remember to buy enough oil to fry the potato latkes?" asked Rosie.

"When I think about your daddy, I remember how much he looks like your Grandpa Reuben," said Grandma.

"I can't remember Grandpa Reuben," said Rosie.

"That's because he died when you were just a little baby," said Grandma. "You were the apple of his eye, Rosie Posie."

"How do Grandpa Reuben and my daddy and wearing inside-out clothes remind you to buy enough oil to fry the potato latkes?" asked Rosie.

"When I think about your daddy and Grandpa Reuben, I think about their coppery red hair," said Grandma.

"I have red hair, too!" cried Rosie. "And roses are red and my name is Rosie! But Grandma, how do red hair and Grandpa Reuben and my daddy and wearing inside-out clothes remind you to buy enough oil to fry the potato latkes?"

"When I think about Grandpa Reuben's red hair, I'm reminded of a shiny new penny," said Grandma. "And that reminds me of my penny jar."

"I've never seen so many pennies in my whole entire life!" cried Rosie. "Are you going to buy the oil with all of these pennies?"

"Oh no, Rosie Posie, these pennies are for the Hanukkah gelt. You remember, that's the present you get for Hanukkah."

Rosie's eyes grew very large. "There must be eighty-nine thousand pennies in this jar!" she said. "But come on, Grandma, please tell me how a jar of Hanukkah gelt and red hair and Grandpa Reuben and my daddy and wearing inside-out clothes remind you to buy enough oil to fry the potato latkes."

"When I think about the jar full of Hanukkah gelt, I remember my papa's silver dreidel," said Grandma, "and how he loved to spin that little silver top."

"Oh, I know! We need the pennies to play the dreidel game," said Rosie.

"That's right," said Grandma. "Of course, when I remember the silver dreidel, I remember our beautiful old Hanukkah menorah.

"I see the burning candles glowing brightly in the faces of our whole family. I see you and your baby brother, Max, your mommy and daddy, your Aunt Natalie, Cousin Eli and the twins. I see your Uncle Russell and his family, the Lupinskys from next door, and Izzy Nachenwurster, the butcher. Since his wife, Sadie, died, he's been alone. Nobody should spend Hanukkah all alone."

"I know that," said Rosie. "But Grandma, my daddy will be here soon and I still don't know how you remember the oil!"

Grandma laughed. "When I see a house full of aunts and uncles and cousins and friends, I think, It's going to take a lot of latkes to feed this crowd!

"Honestly, the way you gobble down those latkes, it's all I can do just to keep up!"

"That's because your potato latkes are the very best latkes in the whole entire world!" raved Rosie. "They're so crunchy and delicious."

"And do you know what it takes to make those latkes so crunchy and delicious?" winked Grandma.

"OIL!" declared Rosie. "Lots and lots of oil!"
Grandma and Rosie laughed and laughed until the doorbell rang.
"I'll get it!" cried Rosie. "I bet it's my daddy."

Daddy gave Rosie a big bear hug, and he gave one to Grandma, too.

"Mama," Daddy said, "do you know that you have your clothes on inside out?"

GRANDMA'S CRUNCHY AND DELICIOUS
POTATO LATKES

3–4 pounds potatoes
1 medium onion for each lb. of potatoes
1 egg
1½ teaspoons salt
½ teaspoon pepper
2 heaping tablespoons matzo meal
  (or just enough to hold the mixture together)
½ teaspoon baking soda

(1) Scrub, but <u>DO NOT PEEL</u>, the potatoes. The skins are full of vitamins and add a hearty flavor.

(2) Grate the potatoes and the onions <u>TOGETHER</u>. This helps keep the potatoes from turning dark. A food processor or grinder makes this job easier!

(3) Allow the mixture to drain and then squeeze out the remaining liquid. Reserve the potato starch (that fine white paste that settles on the bottom) and return it to the mixture.

(4) Add the remaining ingredients.

(5) Drop by spoonfuls onto a hot, <u>WELL-OILED</u> skillet and flatten into nice round pancakes.

(6) Fry on both sides until golden brown and crispy.

(7) When ready, drain the latkes on flattened brown paper bags from the supermarket.

(8) Serve immediately with applesauce and sour cream.

Yield: approximately 24 latkes

Betayavon! (Hearty Appetite!)